THE MYSTERY

AT

Yellowstone National Park

Managing Editor: Sherry Moss
Assistant Editor: Paige Muh
Cover Design: Vicki DeJoy
Content Design: Randolyn Friedlander

Gallopade International is introducing SAT words that kids need to know in each
new book that we publish. The SAT words are bold in the story. Look for this
special logo beside each word in the glossary. Happy Learning!

Gallopade is proud to be a member and supporter of these educational organizations
and associations:

American Booksellers Association
American Library Association
International Reading Association
National Association for Gifted Children
The National School Supply and Equipment Association
The National Council for the Social Studies
Museum Store Association
Association of Partners for Public Lands
Association of Booksellers for Children
Association for the Study of African American Life and History
National Alliance of Black School Educators

Once upon a time...

Hmm, kids keep asking me to write a mystery book. What shall I do?

Mimi

Write one about spiders!

Papa said …

Why don't you set the stories in real locations?

That's a great idea! And if I do that, I might as well choose real kids as characters in the stories! But which kids would I pick?

MiMi, PiCK ME, PiCK ME!

ME, TOO, MiMi, PiCK ME, TOO!

Christina

Grant

Pick me!

6

You two really are characters, that's all I've got to say!

Yes you are! And, of course I choose you! But what should I write about?

National Parks!

SCARY PLACES!

Famous Places!

FUN PLACES!

Disney World!

New York City!

Dracula's Castle

GRAND CANYON

On the *Mystery Girl* airplane ...

I can FLY us anywhere!

Mystery Girl

Or aboard the *Mimi!*

Mimi

Take me to the Forbidden City!

Or by surfboard, rickshaw, motorbike, camel ...

All great ideas! I can put a lot of history, MYSTERY, legend, lore, and laughs in the books! We can use other boys and girls in the books. It will be educational and fun!

Good stuff!

Where will you get the other kids, Mimi?

From my Fan Club! Kids can apply to be characters!

And can you put some cool stuff online? Like a Book Club and a Scavenger Hunt and a Map so we can track our adventures?

Of course!

And can cousins Avery and Ella and Evan and some of our friends be in the books?

Of course!

Can I apply?

*A*nd so, Mimi, Papa, Christina, and Grant took off aboard the *Mystery Girl* and America's National Mystery Book Series—where the adventure is real and so are the characters! —was born.

START YOUR ADVENTURE TODAY!

READ THE BOOK!

GO ONLINE!

Yikes! That was close!

TRACK YOUR ADVENTURES!

APPLY TO BE A CHARACTER!

Rats!

Yellowstone National Park
by Grant

Well, folks, here I am in Cody, Wyyyyoming, 'bout to head West, young man, go West...to Yellowstone! I hear tell is a big, doggone place. I hear tell there's grizzlies... bison...a'bubblin' mud pots...gobs of geysers...snow that steams...and ghostly vapors...and, best of all, there's a SUPERVOLCANO! Well, gotta go get my boots on and my snowmobile warmed up. Mimi and Papa are a'waitin' on cowboy Grant and I don't want to get left behind. Oh, yeah, Christina's coming, too. I just have one question: Should I be scared?

1
BELIEVE IT OR NOT!

Grant began to stir in his rumpled hotel bed sheets, rolling from side to side as he did every morning as he woke up. This morning he had the strange sensation that someone was watching him. He cracked open one eye to see a small lens right in front of his face.

"Christina! What are you doing?" Grant croaked. His sister was standing directly over him with her brand new video camera pointing down at him. Grant whipped the sheet over his head and buried down deep into his feather bed.

"Gooood morning, little brother! It's a marvelous day for a snowmobile ride!" Christina turned her camera toward the window and began filming the snow-covered rolling hills of Cody, Wyoming. "Wow! I can't believe that some people get to look at this view every day. It sure is different than little ol' Peachtree City, Georgia."

Grant slowly crawled out of the covers and sat upright. He rubbed his fingers over his face and through his tousled blond hair. "The only scenery I want to see right now is a loaded breakfast buffet," he said. "I hope they serve real sourdough pancakes out here in the West!"

Christina and Grant had arrived in Cody the night before, along with their grandparents, Mimi and Papa. The kids often traveled with their grandparents while Mimi did research for the children's mystery books she wrote. Mimi always said that the ability to give her grandchildren excitement AND an education was the best job in the world!

Wyoming was one of Papa's favorite parts of the country. One of his fondest memories was a snowmobile tour of Yellowstone National Park that he and Mimi had taken years earlier. A cowboy through and through, Papa was excited to recreate that expedition for his grandchildren. The stop in Cody was a brief layover on the way to what Papa described as a "journey through one of the United States' most valuable treasures." He couldn't wait to put on his cowboy hat and boots and share that treasure with Grant and Christina.

There was a knock at the door adjoining the kids' room to their grandparents' suite.

"Kiddos! You up?" Papa hollered. "We've gotta get a move on—mud pots and geysers and bison await!"

"We're up, Papa!" replied Christina. "We're getting our snow bibs on and packing up our stuff." Christina and Grant loved to snow ski every year with their parents, so luckily they had all the cold weather clothing they would need on this tour. Snowmobiling through the park would be all kinds of fun—but since Yellowstone gets an average of 150 inches of snow every year, it would also be all kinds of cold!

Christina stowed her video camera in her backpack. The kids quickly got dressed, gathered their things, and headed to meet Mimi and Papa for breakfast. They were looking forward to filling up with food, and also filling up with the details Papa and Mimi would give them about their trip.

"Papa, when are we getting our snowmobiles?" Grant asked. "I've been practicing my driving skills on my video game. I'm ready to speed all around the trails!" He plopped down at the restaurant table with Frisbee-sized pancakes and greasy bacon spilling off his plate.

Christina's eyes got huge as she put granola and fruit into her yogurt. She had heard there were dangers to look out for throughout the national park, but she never thought it would be her brother on a snowmobile! Luckily, Papa quickly put her mind at ease.

"Oh, I don't think so, cowboy!" Papa said. "You must have a driver's license to operate a snowmobile. The last time I checked, you didn't have one. So you will be RIDING—not driving on this trip."

As Papa piloted the *Mystery Girl* to Cody the night before, Christina sat in the back of the plane finishing up a fantastic book she'd begun reading that very morning, so she hadn't yet asked her grandmother what this winter excursion was all about.

"Ok, Mimi," Christina began, "what's so great about Yellowstone? Why do you and Papa love it so much?"

"Yeah, Mimi," said Grant, "we've been to a national park before. Why is this one any different?"

Mimi pulled her sparkly glasses from her face and smiled at her grandson. "Grant, Yellowstone isn't just *A* national park. It is *THE* national park—the very first national park in the entire world."

"All thanks to President Ulysses S. Grant," said Papa. "He realized that the land and the water and the wildlife here were valuable to the world. So in 1872, he declared that the area would be a national park. As it says on the Roosevelt Arch up at the North Entrance of the park, 'Yellowstone is for the benefit and enjoyment of the people.'"

"So what are we going to see?" asked Christina, popping a last grape into her mouth. "Oh, Christina," said Mimi, "the park is full of sights and sounds and smells that you could never imagine!"

"That's right," said Papa. "As a matter of fact, when the 19th century explorers began telling the stories about what they saw in this wilderness, people didn't believe them."

"What couldn't they believe?" asked Grant skeptically.

"They couldn't believe what you are getting ready to see on this trip," said Mimi. "Yellowstone National Park is a boiling, bubbling, steaming, gushing, spewing, sizzling, smelly place!"

Grant looked out the window at the sun coming up and glistening off the powder-white snow. "It's freezing cold and there is a ton of snow outside," he said. "I don't see how anything can boil and steam in the dead of winter."

"That's what's so amazing about Yellowstone, young 'un," said Papa. "And wait until you see the wildlife—oh, the animals we'll see! Bison, bears, deer, wolves, elk, coyotes, eagles..." his voice trailed off.

Mimi loved to see Papa's eyes light up and the permanent grin attach to his face when he was out in this part of the country.

Christina grabbed her video camera out of her backpack and hit the 'Record' button. "Land that is boiling and steaming? This I gotta see! And film, of course!" she said. "So when do we start?"

"If Grant will wipe that syrup off his chin, we can start right now!" said Papa. "We'll commandeer some snowmobiles and be on our way!"

Grant was excited but also a bit skeptical. As he zipped up his heavy coat and headed to the door with his sister and his grandparents, he secretly hoped that something interesting would crop up during their trip that would add a little thrill to their journey!

He wouldn't have to wait long.

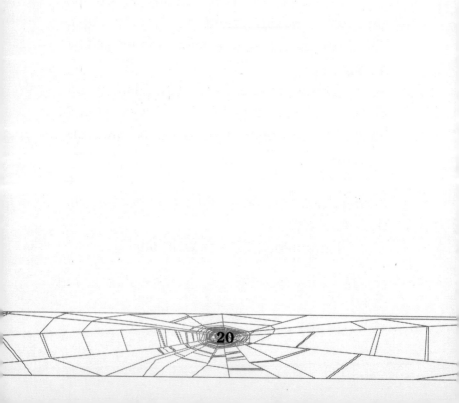

2
REPETITIVE ROUTES

Molly Jane Edwards put rubber bands around her hair braids, stuck her glasses on her face, and let out a sigh. Every year Molly Jane and her parents made the same trip from their house in Jackson Hole, Wyoming to Yellowstone National Park. Her parents were obsessed with the place! For hours, they would watch the mud pots bubble and belch. Or they'd examine and analyze the churning, swirling hot springs and thermal pools or spewing geysers. Her dad could explain how algae could change the color of the water as it tumbled over the Lower Falls, the highest waterfall in the park. Her mom loved the wildflowers and the trees in spring and would

continuously chirp out their names in English and in Latin!

Without even realizing it, Molly Jane had become something of an expert of the science behind the sights and sounds of Yellowstone. Her parents were great teachers and it was hard not to get swept up in their excitement about these natural wonders, even as they were headed to Flagg Ranch at the park's South Entrance for the sixth time in as many years.

At least this time would be a little different since they were going in the middle of winter. Molly was excited that they would be traveling by snow coach instead of by car. Hopefully there wouldn't be as many traffic jams with snowmobiles and snow coaches as there were with cars during the height of tourist season. Maybe the snow and the trails would shed new light on some of these places in Yellowstone that she knew so well.

If only I had a friend to go with me this time, thought Molly Jane. If only there was a new way to look at the park or a more interesting way to experience its sights. Little did she know there were other kids headed to Yellowstone with the exact same idea!

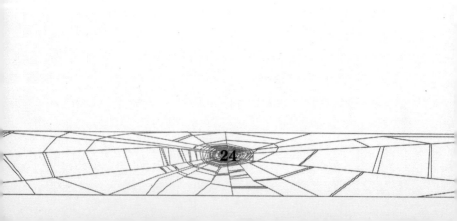

3

SURPRISE SURPRISE!

Gunny Mitchell's great-great-grandfather was a world-class hiker back in his day. He had traveled through some of the most scenic and most dangerous areas in the entire United States, documenting his travels in his journals. His expeditions were revered among hikers to this very day.

"Remind me, Dad, if great-great-grandfather James was such a good hiker, then why did he die by falling into a hot spring at Yellowstone?" Gunny asked his father as they were packing up their camping gear.

"It was an unfortunate accident, Gunny," replied his father. "He stumbled into a spring while hiking at night. Back in those days, the hot springs at Yellowstone were not marked. If it was dark and someone could not see where they were walking, they could fall in and die a very gruesome death. The water in hot springs can be more than 200 degrees Fahrenheit."

Gunny shuddered. He had burned his fingers on a hot roll the night before—he couldn't imagine what 200 degrees would feel like!

Gunny and his dad were driving down to the North Entrance of Yellowstone from Bozeman, Montana. Mr. Mitchell was an animal researcher, **specializing** in wildlife of the West—bison, elk, moose, and bears especially. Because of his dad, Gunny loved the outdoors and the animals that lived there. Gunny was big and strong for his age, the perfect size for a middle school kid who helped his father on wildlife research trips. Mr. Mitchell was documenting winter habitats of endangered wildlife in Yellowstone and offered to take Gunny along with him. When they reached the North Entrance, he surprised Gunny with the fact that they would be taking snowmobiles through the park to have a little fun while they were working.

Mr. Mitchell would have been surprised himself if he had known what Gunny had planned. In the attic of their house, the boy had found a faded Yellowstone trail map scribbled with notes, lines, and markings that obviously belonged to his great-great-grandfather James. There was a note attached to the front that read:

> If you have this map, then I am no longer hiking this earth.
> To you, I leave clues to something more valuable than gold;
> More precious than gems; a treasure of a lifetime.
> Its owner will only profit from its riches!

Gunny had the map and the note hidden in his backpack (his father jokingly referred to it as his "Gunny Sack"). He didn't want to tell his dad that he had other ideas about their trip through Yellowstone because he knew his father's research was important. But maybe, just maybe, he could do a little treasure hunting while they were there. He wished he was an expert at following clues because the first clue already had him stumped. Maybe he would run into tourists or park rangers who could help him, he thought.

4

CALDERA CONFUSION CONUNDRUM

As their snowmobiles sailed across the trails into the park, Christina looked out over the hills and fields and couldn't believe her eyes. Everywhere she looked, white steam and mist rose from the ground like a ghostly fog. She could see large streams winding their way through the fields, iced-over trees dotting the hillsides, and snowcapped mountains in the distance.

And visible in and out of the thick steam was wildlife—in packs and pairs and singles. There were brown, hulking bison, and pointy-antlered mule deer, scurrying ground squirrels, and pika. The fields were teeming with animal activity.

Grant must have noticed the thick white clouds seeping out of the ground, too. Tugging hard on his grandfather's coat, he became panicked. "Papa! Papa!" he screamed, barely audible over the snowmobile engine and the wind streaming past them.

Papa came to a snow-spraying halt.

"Papa! Smoke! Look!" he cried. To Grant, it seemed as if the entire field must be on fire. "How can SNOW be on fire, Papa?" he asked.

"That's not fire, Grant. That is steam rising from the hot springs and vents, or fumaroles, that are everywhere in Yellowstone," explained Papa, taking off his helmet.

"Hot spring? But it's not spring, it's winter!" said Grant.

"Not the season, Grant," corrected Papa. "I mean HOT springs—sometimes very hot water that has come to the surface after having been heated by magma below the surface—well at least that's what creates them here at Yellowstone. Let's get to Yellowstone

Lake and I'll explain." With that, the snowmobilers zoomed on through the wilderness.

A short time later, the kids found themselves standing on the shore of Yellowstone Lake, the crystal blue water covered in ice as far as they could see.

"This lake looks almost as big as the ocean! Is it completely frozen over?" asked Christina. She could feel the wind biting her face as it whipped across North America's largest, high-elevation lake and she struggled to hold her video camera steady.

Out of the corner of his eye, Grant caught a glimpse of an otter scampering across a frozen portion of water and then diving into a hole in the ice. "Well, not completely frozen over," he said. "Hey, why are some parts of the lake frozen but some parts melted, Mimi?"

"For the same reason that Yellowstone is such a special place, Grant," said Mimi. "Underneath the entire park is a volcano, some even say a 'supervolcano'!"

"VOLCANO?!?!" screamed Grant. "RUN FOR YOUR LIVES! MOLTEN LAVA ON ITS WAY!!" Grant shoved his helmet on his head and began to sprint for Papa's snowmobile.

Papa caught Grant in the crook of his arm and reeled him back into the group. With a hearty laugh, Papa explained, "A volcano hasn't erupted here in over 600,000 years, my boy. I assure you we are safe today!" Grant grimaced at his grandfather.

"Yellowstone wasn't formed overnight. In fact, this park took two million years to create—it was a combination of glacier movement, flooding, erosion, and volcanic eruptions!" said Mimi. "The eruptions were so enormous and violent that the center of the volcano collapsed in on itself because there was nothing left underneath it. What was left is a landscape called a caldera, which filled up with water to form Yellowstone Lake. And even though the volcano itself has collapsed, hot molten magma still runs under the surface."

Christina swung her video around to film her grandmother. "Bu[t]" she said, "in school we studied tha[t] runs under the entire earth's surfa[ce]. [Why] should that be any different here?"

"Because," began Mimi, "instead of it being 25 to 30 miles underneath the earth's surface, as it is everywhere else in the world, at Yellowstone the magma is only 3 to 8 miles beneath the surface. Pretty different, right?!?!"

"I'd say!" exclaimed Grant. "So the heat from the magma makes the steam that we saw on our way here?"

"Exactly," said Papa, impressed. "Ground water mixes with the heat from the magma to create steam. That steam heat escapes through openings in the earth's surface."

"Ok, ok—enough geology for right now!" promised Mimi. "You will understand more when we get to the geysers, other hot springs, and boiling mud pots!"

Grant relaxed since his grandfather assured him that his life wasn't in imminent danger from an erupting volcano. He looked around at the mountains in the distance, at the snow all around, and realized how COLD it was here on the earth's surface next to Yellowstone Lake. "Sure wish I had a little magma to warm me up right now!" he said.

"You could hop into Yellowstone Lake," suggested Papa. "Even though the top of the lake is frozen over, the bottom of the lake is probably boiling like a pot of spaghetti because of the hot springs beneath it!"

"Well, I'm not going to the bottom of that lake," said Mimi, "but I am going to the snowmobile to use those feet and hand warmers!" Papa followed to keep her company while she warmed up.

Christina filmed Grant as he wandered around the shore of the lake. They had not noticed that a snowmobile and a snow coach had joined them in the picnic area.

But was that good news or bad in this lonesome winterscape?

5
A SLOW-SNOW FENDER-BENDER

After about 20 minutes of exploration along the shore of icy Yellowstone Lake, Mimi insisted that they get on their way. She said they needed to stay on schedule, but Grant knew she just wanted to keep her feet in the foot warmers.

Papa and Grant turned their snowmobile to head back to the trail, but Mimi and Christina didn't follow. Instead of moving forward, the girls went in reverse! The back end of Mimi's snowmobile crunched into the front end of an orange snowmobile that carried a man and a boy. The orange snowmobile knocked into the snow coach sitting alongside it. It was a snowpack pile-up!

A girl about Christina's age ran over when she saw the commotion.

"Bison burgers!" griped Mimi, yanking off her helmet.

Papa bolted to Mimi's side and several adults gathered around to discuss whatever adults discuss in messy situations like an unexpected fender-bender.

Grant watched as the boy hopped off the back of the orange snowmobile and trotted through the snow toward Christina and the girl. Cool! More kids, thought Grant, and he scampered over to join them.

"Are you ok?" Christina asked the boy. "Oh, sure!" he replied. "It takes a lot more than that to bother me!"

"Now that's the kind of excitement we usually have on our trips!" exclaimed Grant. "It's not a trip with Mimi and Papa unless something nutty happens! Hi! I'm Grant and this is my sister Christina and that was our grandmother who just rammed into you!"

Gunny introduced himself to Christina and Grant. "It's cool you have a snowmobiling grandma!"

"I'm Molly Jane," said the girl who had run to the scene, "and that's my family's snow coach that got whacked, too."

Gunny got an immediate feeling about these kids. They seemed like they could be just the help he was looking for to decipher his great-great-grandfather's treasure map. "If it is true that you like excitement, I think I've got a great idea! Are you guys interested in solving some mysterious clues to find a hidden treasure somewhere here in Yellowstone?"

Christina smiled to herself, amazed that a mystery could find them even in the middle of snow-covered Yellowstone National Park. Before she could answer, her brother was bouncing up and down and answering for both of them.

"Clues? Mystery? Treasure? We're in!" squealed Grant. "Who cares about erupting volcanoes when we've got HIDDEN TREASURE!"

On the outside, Molly Jane acted uncertain about such an adventure, but on the inside, her stomach flipped joyfully. This was more than she could have hoped for. If anyone could help with clues around Yellowstone, she could.

"This is my sixth trip to Yellowstone. I'm pretty sure I could help!" she offered.

"Great!" said Gunny, pulling the map out of his sack. He told the kids about his great-great-grandfather's background, and then read them the cryptic note. Unfolding the map, he continued, "Here is the first clue. Maybe it means something to one of you, because it makes no sense to me."

At the top of the trail map, scrawled in smudged pencil lead were the words:

GO WEST THUMB, YOUNG MAN! GO WEST THUMB!

"Thumb?" said Grant. He raised his hands in the air and with a goofy grin, gave the two-thumbs-up signal to the other kids, who giggled.

"Hmmm," mumbled Christina, rolling her eyes at her silly brother.

"How about this?" he continued and stuck out a hitchhiker's thumb and pretended like he was looking for a ride.

"Grant!" said Christina, exasperated.

"Just trying to help!" said Grant.

Gunny couldn't help but laugh. "I'll take any help I can get! I'm 'all thumbs' when it comes to figuring out clues."

"Ok, Gunny, let me see that map," instructed Molly Jane. "I think I may have the answer to this first clue."

The kids moved to a nearby picnic table, brushed away the snow, and gathered around the map. Molly Jane moved her finger over the map, looking for something specific. Then her finger came to a stop.

"Here!" she said. "West Thumb! It's a geyser basin right on Yellowstone Lake."

"That sounds great," said Christina, "but that also sounds like a big problem."

Simultaneously, the four kids looked over at the group of adults milling around the jumble of snow vehicles. Each of them knew that the real challenge would be convincing the grown-ups to set out on a treasure hunt, without even realizing it.

6
NO SWIMMING IN THESE POOLS!

Before the kids could devise a plan to set out for West Thumb, the adults handed one to them.

Mimi, a man in a Yellowstone National Park ranger uniform, Molly Jane's mother, and Gunny's dad walked over to where the kids were standing at the picnic table. Gunny noticed the park ranger was staring at the map, so he quickly folded it up and stowed it in his snow bib. The oversized ranger, whose name tag read MAGNUS, stared at Gunny with a **menacing** look. Gunny looked away quickly.

"Luckily, our new friends here are very understanding," said Mimi, motioning toward

Mr. Mitchell and Mrs. Edwards. "I think we've come up with a good idea to help them with this slight inconvenience."

When Grant looked puzzled, Christina whispered to him, "She means this big mess of snow and smashed vehicles!"

Mr. Mitchell looked at Gunny and said, "The Edwards and I will go with Ranger Magnus here to the ranger station to get replacement vehicles."

All the kids looked stricken, as if they had just heard the worst news of their lives. Their treasure-hunting group that had just formed was now being disbanded by force.

Mimi, in her red parka and matching hat, piped up to save the day. "Even though my snowmobile caused this ruckus, it's running fine. Papa and I have offered to take Molly Jane and Gunny with us, so they can enjoy the park while the adults get new transportation. Of course, that's only if you kids want to join us?"

"Sure!" said Molly Jane. Treasure hunt or not, it would be more fun to be with her new friends today.

"Sounds great to me!" said Gunny, smiling at Grant and Christina. At least this would give them more time to devise a plan to get to West Thumb, and that creepy Magnus would be doing his job somewhere else, and not sneaking any more looks at the map.

Heading to the trails at West Thumb Geyser Basin with the other kids, Grant called out to his grandparents, "Can we go exploring on our own, Mimi and Papa?"

"You may," said Papa, "but you must stay on the boardwalks and no running or horseplay! One stumble or step in the wrong direction and you'll be swimming in a pool you don't ever want to be in—unless you want to be a fried shrimp. Be safe." The couple headed off to take pictures for Mimi's upcoming book.

The kids made their way to the frozen, slushy wooden boardwalk that surrounded the pools of hot springs and geysers that made up West Thumb Geyser Basin. Out in the distance, they could see the frozen water of Yellowstone Lake, but all around them was water of a very different sort. There were pools of blue water in all shapes and sizes, some steaming like hot cocoa, others bubbling like hot stew. Snow had melted away from the areas that rimmed the hot pools.

"Why does a geyser spew water in the air and a hot spring just bubble?" Christina wondered aloud, standing over the steaming turquoise blue and emerald green waters of Blue Funnel Springs.

"It's all about temperature and the amount of water that is in the ground," said Molly Jane, remembering what her parents taught her. "In a hot spring, there's a lot of water but the temperature is not as hot as in a geyser. The heat from the ground is continuously released through the boiling water and steam."

Molly Jane shuffled with Christina through the snow over to Twin Geysers. "In a geyser, there is a lot of water AND extremely high temperatures. That mixture creates so much pressure under the ground that the heat explodes through the top of the geyser, spraying the water, steam, and usually rock and dirt straight to the sky!"

"Sounds like what happens when you shake a soda pop bottle really hard and then open it—it becomes a soda geyser!" said Christina.

The kids explored the steaming springs and the bubbling pools, each with its own set of magnificent color combinations—mustard yellows, bright greens, sky blues; and each with its own voice—gurgling, plopping, hiccupping, percolating.

"That water just burped!" squealed Grant, pointing to Surging Springs as its waves overflowed into Yellowstone Lake. He and Gunny began a burping contest in honor of the noises from the spring.

"Ok, you two!" said Christina, trying to bring a stop to the disgusting noises coming from the boys. "Let's try to follow the clue. What are we looking for?"

Gunny pulled the map out of his snow bib and gave it a glance. "West Thumb is enormous," he said. "Where should we start?"

With her video camera, Christina began to film the steam billowing out of one of the pools. She turned and zoomed in close on Gunny's map. And that's when she saw something she hadn't noticed before.

"Look at this symbol," she said, turning off the camera and pointing to the corner of the map nearest the written clue. In a dark red color, four triangles formed a shape that resembled a star. In between each triangle, a line emerged that made the star look as if it were shining brightly.

"I never paid much attention to that," admitted Gunny. "Maybe that's what we're looking for. If we find that symbol, then maybe we will find the treasure or at least another clue."

Molly Jane loved this! She had been up and down this boardwalk many times before, but now it looked completely different. It looked like a place that was hiding a clue to a treasure. She stomped through the snow-covered walkway ahead of the other kids and began searching the boardwalk railings and the signs that named the different pools beneath.

Christina and Grant walked down the boardwalk directly beside Yellowstone Lake. They stopped to look at a rock with a hole in the center jutting out of the ice.

An old, salty dog of a man was standing nearby. "You like fishin'?" he asked the kids.

"Sure," answered Grant. "I sometimes fish with my Papa!"

"Well, this is my favorite fishin' spot in the whole world," the old man said. "But it's been a long time since I fished here."

"How come?" asked Grant, wondering if this man had a grandson to take fishing, too.

"See that rock right there?" he asked. "It's called Fishing Cone. And used to be that you could catch a trout on your hook and then stick that fish—hook and all—straight into its boiling water. Then—'ta-da'—you'd have cooked trout for dinner without even taking it off the line! Now, fishing is not allowed here."

Christina and Grant laughed—knowing that would be Papa's favorite fishing spot, too!

Christina joined Molly Jane again. She was standing behind a young couple reading a sign with a toddler at the end of a leash attached to his mother's belt loop.

"My parents used to put me on a leash at Yellowstone when I was small," said Molly Jane, noticing the child at the end of the tether. "Parents shouldn't take their eyes off their little kids even for a minute. It's too easy for a little kid to fall off the boardwalk and into a burning hot spring."

"Does that happen often?" Christina asked. She took a giant step away from the nearest pool as it gurgled and bubbled.

"Not often," said Molly Jane, "but it happens. My dad has this book called *Death in Yellowstone*, and you wouldn't believe the stupid ways people find to cook themselves here in the park."

"Or get gobbled by a grizzly," added Gunny.

"As in bear?" asked Grant, looking nervously over his shoulder.

"As in BEAR!" promised Gunny.

Christina wished she had eyes in the back of her head the way Mimi always swore she did. She thought she'd better keep a keener eye out for treasure, tripping, and bear tracks!

The kids walked on down the boardwalk and the girls moved up to look at the next sign. It said THERMAL GARDENS and explained how plant life could live around the thermal features of the pools. But that's not what the girls saw. At the same time, they both noticed the small triangle star formation at the bottom of the sign

"Grant! Gunny!" Molly Jane yelled. "Come quick!"

"What did you find?" said Grant, running up to the girls, Gunny close behind.

"There's the symbol," said Christina, pointing. "Now where is our clue?"

"Or our treasure?" said Gunny.

"In my experience," said Christina, "a hidden treasure will probably not be found after just one clue." She began running her hands along the wooden railing of the boardwalk in front of the sign.

Gunny looked skeptical, but Grant reassured him, "Trust her on this, Gunny.

She knows what she's talking about. We've done this kind of thing before!"

Just as Grant finished his sentence, Christina's finger found a knothole on the underside of the railing. She slid her finger in as far as she could, and sure enough, pulled out a small scrap of paper.

Christina turned the paper over to see if something was written on it. Faded and barely legible, she read:

PAINT FROM THE FOUNTAIN!

"Oh, great," huffed Grant. "I knew I should have paid more attention in art class. I can't even paint a wall!"

"Are there fountains in Yellowstone?" asked Christina.

"I saw a water fountain back at that picnic area," said Grant.

"I bet we aren't looking for a real fountain," said Molly Jane. "I bet the clue is talking about the Fountain Paint Pot."

"Who wants to see a pot of paint?" asked Grant, unimpressed.

"It's not really paint, Grant," said Molly. "It's actually mud. The steam from below the ground heats up the surface water on top and the tiny microbes break down the rocks to form the muddy clay. The reason they call it a paint pot is because the minerals and other stuff in the rocks and mud make the pretty colors."

"You sure know a lot about this place, Molly Jane," said Christina admiringly.

"I told you, I've been here a bunch of times. My parents are big fans of all these crazy thermal features around this park," Molly Jane said, half embarrassed, half proud.

As the kids discussed the location and how to get to Fountain Paint Pot, Mimi, Papa, and Ranger Magnus walked up to join the group. Gunny was not happy to see the ranger staring right at him. Gunny looked at Christina and hoped she would understand his look that meant "HIDE THAT CLUE!" but she didn't. Ranger Magnus noticed the paper in Christina's hand and was obviously distracted by it.

"Ranger Magnus was nice enough to check on us and make sure our snowmobile was running ok," Mimi said. Mimi always appreciated when bigwigs made sure their trips were running smoothly.

"It's not every day that our park hosts the great mystery book writer Carole Marsh!" Ranger Magnus said. "I don't want there to be anything mysterious about your time with us."

"No mysteries here, Ranger," said Papa. He looked at his grandchildren sternly as if to say "there had better NOT be any!"

The kids looked at one another sheepishly.

As they walked back to the snowmobiles, Gunny quietly told Christina about how Ranger Magnus seemed overly interested in the map and the clue they just found.

"He gives me the creeps," said Gunny.

Red flags were going off in Christina's head. Perhaps they weren't the only ones interested in hidden treasure at Yellowstone.

7
A CONTINENT DIVIDED

The two snowmobiles cruised along the snow-plowed roads through the lodgepole pine trees that looked like toothpicks with white icing. Birds flew low overhead, hoping to find a scampering chipmunk or red squirrel for a late afternoon snack.

Mimi followed Papa's snowmobile off to the side of the road near a huge park sign that said: CONTINENTAL DIVIDE.

"What are we doing here?" asked Grant. "This looks like the boonies!"

Papa stood up straight in the stance he took when he was about to explain something that was always educational but not always interesting to his grandkids. Christina decided to film him regardless of the outcome and pulled out her video camera.

"We are standing on the Continental Divide," began Papa.

"What's it dividing?" asked Grant. "And WHO decided to divide it?"

"The Continental Divide is a ridge of mountains within the Rocky Mountains that extend through North America, north to south," said Papa. "It separates the rivers and streams that flow west into the Pacific Ocean from the ones that flow east into the Atlantic Ocean."

Christina and Molly Jane stood and looked out over the divide to see if there was a drop-off or change in the landscape. But here it all looked about the same, like when you cross from one state to another when you're traveling on the interstate. Nothing looked different.

To entertain himself, Grant stood next to the CONTINENTAL DIVIDE sign, jumped in front of it and said, "I'm a river and I'm flowing east!"

He jumped behind the sign and said, "Now I'm flowing west!"

He continued jumping back and forth in front of and behind the sign shouting, "Now east! Now west! Now east! Now west!" over and over again.

Everyone groaned at Grant's silliness and headed back to the snowmobiles.

Grant giggled to himself and then started to reach into his coat pocket to warm his hands when all of a sudden—his pocket moved!

"Hey, what's going on?" Grant asked out loud to his pocket. Suddenly, a hamster-sized baby squirrel poked its head out of Grant's coat pocket. While Grant was jumping back and forth at the park sign, the squirrel must have scurried into Grant's coat to find some leftover toast from this morning's breakfast buffet.

"Ok, you little thief," cried Grant, pulling the pocket-critter out in the open. "I guess you'll eat more than twigs and leaves today!" The furry rodent leaped from Grant's hand and scampered off with its prize.

After filming the baby squirrel running away, Christina put away her video camera and climbed back on the snowmobile. It was then that she thought she saw Ranger Magnus pass them on an official Yellowstone National Park snowmobile and give a slight nod of his head.

Was he keeping an eye on them, she wondered. And if so, why? Yellowstone was a mighty big park for them to keep coincidentally running into one another, she thought.

8

THE SMELL FROM YOU KNOW WHERE!

The kids, with the boys in the lead, were excited to see whatever they could around Fountain Paint Pots, and hopefully find that symbol that would lead them to a clue.

The azure blue waters of the Celestine Pool and Silex Springs were steaming and bubbling as they moved passed them down the boardwalk. A fly landed on Grant's nose as he walked past the pools. He swatted it away, only for it to set down on his nose again a few seconds later.

"All right, you pest!" said Grant with another swat. "Beat it!" And with that, a swarm of flies surrounded him. Grant's arms flailed everywhere as he tried to keep the flies away. "Aaaaggghh! I'm being attacked!" he yelped.

Grant ran forward, flapping his arms like a bird until he was able to outrun the pesky insects. "Where did they come from?" he said to no one in particular.

A man with a University of Wisconsin emblem on his coat turned to look at Grant. "Those flies love the bacteria that lives in these hot springs," he said.

"Yuck! Bacteria-eating flies!" said Grant, as he caught his breath. "I thought flies only liked to eat picnic food."

"Well, this is pretty special bacteria," said the man. "I'm a doctor of medical research at a large university and we use the bacteria that is found in these very pools to help find ways to treat medical conditions. Those flies love a bacteria that has been part of some very important scientific discoveries."

"Wow," Grant said. "My mom always tells me to wash my hands to get rid of bacteria. I'll have to tell her that it just might be good for me!"

The doctor continued, "The bacteria is only good for those of us in scientific research...and of course, for these flies. You keep washing your hands like your mom says!"

As Christina walked through these hot springs and other natural wonders, she couldn't help but notice a man-made feature—a sign that said:

•UNSTABLE GROUND •BOILING WATER

•STAY ON DESIGNATED TRAILS

OR WALKWAYS

The sign made her a little more on edge. To be so beautiful, Yellowstone certainly is dangerous.

When they made the turn up the hill toward the Fountain Paint Pot, a grimace crossed each kid's face. Molly Jane began laughing and screwing up her nose at the same time.

"EEEEWWWWWW!!" shrieked Grant. "What is that smell?!?" He yanked his heavy coat over his face in an attempt to block it out.

"Gross!!" exclaimed Gunny. "It smells like rotten eggs or something! What IS that?"

Christina had one hand on her video camera and one hand holding her nose. "Oh my gosh! Molly Jane, where is that smell coming from?"

"It's the mud pot!" Molly Jane explained. "There is a gas in the mud pot called hydrogen sulfide and it stinks! You can actually smell it a little bit in all the thermal areas of the park—but the mud pots are the worst!"

"You can say that again!" said Grant, still covering almost his entire face with his coat. He and Gunny exchanged glances and shook their heads in smelly defeat.

The kids did their best to **tolerate** the stench that was everywhere as they explored the area around Fountain Paint Pots. It was an eerie world. Besides the foul smell, the pots were full of gloppy, gurgling mud in an array of colors—yellows, oranges, pinks, and browns. Around the rim of the pit, the earth was scorched and dead.

Thermal features met them at every turn. Molly Jane was thrilled to be able to show off some of her scientific knowledge to the other kids, explaining why geysers spouted, mud pots bubbled, and fumaroles hissed.

Along the boardwalk, Grant came to a stop at one of the rare green trees that bordered the walkway. Looking down where the tree trunk was buried into the earth, he noticed a rock with jagged markings on it. When he focused a little harder, he realized that the jagged markings were in the shape of the triangle star!

"Holy Paint Pot! There it is!" he exclaimed.

The kids quickly focused on where Grant was pointing.

"We can't reach that rock from the boardwalk," said Gunny.

"I'll just slide off the side of the walkway and grab it," suggested Grant. "If the ground is strong enough to hold a tree, it is strong enough to hold me."

"NO!" screamed Christina and Molly Jane together.

"No way, Grant!" said his big sister. "There are signs everywhere around that say we have to stay on the boardwalk, that the ground is not safe. Mimi and Papa would be mortified if we didn't follow the rules and someone got hurt."

Gunny grabbed a long branch that had fallen off a tree and used it to bring the rock closer to the walkway. "I got it!" he shouted, and flipped the rock over for everyone to see. There was something scratched into the bottom of the rock! It said:

It was clearly mystery afoot...a HOT foot!

9
TREE HOUSE OF HORROR

Mimi announced it was time to head for the Old Faithful Snow Lodge, the newest of the park's full-service hotels. But on the way there, she wanted to take a side trip.

"Do you remember when we stayed at the Old Faithful Inn that one spring a few years back?" Mimi asked Papa.

"Do I ever!" Papa replied. "That was some vacation we had! I believe that was the first time I ever came face to face with a coyote! And I just loved watching Old Faithful every day. What I wouldn't give to be able to see Old Faithful from the Inn right now. What a sight!"

"Well, I was just on the phone with Gunny's parents," Mimi remarked. "The cell phone reception wasn't that great, but I'm pretty sure we don't need to meet them at the lodge for a couple of hours."

"So," said Papa, "the Old Faithful Inn isn't open in the winter, but you want to go by there since we have some extra time, right?"

"Well, it's not that far from here by snowmobile," Mimi said. "And, besides. . ."

"I know, you'd like to go there for your research, right?" Papa asked with a big grin.

"Exactly!" Mimi exclaimed.

Christina had stuck the rock clue into her backpack to bring to their hotel. The kids didn't have a chance to talk about the clue before Mimi and Papa had shuffled them off on their next adventure. The mystery would have to wait until later.

Christina and Grant followed Mimi and Papa across the parking lot toward the biggest log cabin they had ever seen. Christina thought it looked like a gingerbread house made of wood, except this gingerbread house looked deserted. Snow seemed to cover every inch of the Inn, except for one thing—the front door stood wide open, and a flickering light flooded the front porch. The sign loomed large above the entrance:

WELCOME
OLD FAITHFUL INN

"Well, look at that," Papa said, as the group stepped off their snowmobiles. "Maybe someone is doing some work on the Inn during the winter. Let's go!"

Grant's mouth fell open when he stepped into the lobby of the Old Faithful Inn. "This is a real live TREE HOUSE!" he squealed.

The lobby was a wide-open space where Grant could see straight up to the logs that formed the roof of the building. Everywhere he looked, gnarled, twisted wood and logs created the interiors—the balconies and stairs and railings that led to the rooms. In the center of the lobby was an enormous stone fireplace and chimney that reached up to the third floor balcony.

"Kids, the man who built this inn back in 1904 was named Robert Reamer," Papa said. "You know, they say he loved this place so much that his ghost still roams the hallways at night."

"Maybe he's the one who left the door open for us because I don't see anybody around here," Grant said. Papa and Mimi had already started for the giant window and didn't hear Grant.

Christina's left eyebrow rose as she looked at her brother. "Mimi and Papa seem to have forgotten that we're in an inn that is supposed to be closed for the winter," Christina said. Grant and Christina looked over at their grandparents. They were rubbing the condensation from the window and trying to make out the Old Faithful Geyser in the fading light.

After almost no begging, which surprised Christina and Grant, their grandparents let them explore the Inn on their own. The last words the children heard Papa say before taking off were, "This place looks completely different than it did in the spring!"

"I'm looking for Robert Reamer's ghost!" admitted Grant, heading to a set of knotty pine stairs and bounding up.

"Not by yourself, you're not!" said Christina, following close behind.

They each took separate stairs to the second floor balcony and then up to the third. The large candlelight fixtures that hung down added spooky shadows to the already sinister wood shapes all around them.

The kids explored all the nooks and crannies that the inn offered—and since it is the largest log structure in the world—there were lots of places for them to look.

"We better head back," suggested Christina after a long while. "You know Mimi and Papa are probably looking for us at this very moment!"

"Alright," Grant agreed reluctantly. "But I didn't see any sign of Robert Reamer's ghost!"

"Grant, you don't seriously think there's a ghost roaming around here, do you?" asked Christina. She always tried to be the voice of reason with her brother, even when she didn't quite believe it herself.

"I guess not," he replied, disappointed. He glanced up at a large, wrought iron tower clock in the center of the lobby. Just then, the clock struck midnight.

"Midnight? That can't be right!" Christina whispered.

The kids tiptoed along the knotty pine balcony. They froze. Right before them, a short, ghostly figure stopped briefly as if listening to the clock, then turned without seeing them, and walked down the hallway with purpose.

10

OH, GIVE ME A HOME, WHERE THE BUF–I MEAN BISON–ROAM

Papa woke them up at the crack of dawn. The sun was barely awake, and here they were already standing at the edge of a snowy Hayden Valley field that extended for miles around them. Last night seemed more like a dream, and Christina started to doubt that it had ever happened! She saw Grant's tired face, but decided against bringing it up. Gunny and Molly Jane were with them in the field this morning, while Mr. Mitchell met with wildlife experts at Yellowstone Lake and the Edwards enjoyed one of their favorite tours around Roosevelt Arch at the North Entrance of the park.

While Mimi and Papa discussed the best spot for wildlife watching, the four kids wandered off on their own.

"Look at all those buffalo," said Christina. "They are everywhere around this park!"

Gunny replied, "Actually, those are bison," he said. "A lot of people think they are buffalo—but bison are different from buffalo. Bison have the huge hump on their back and buffalo don't. Come on, let's go check them out."

The kids traipsed across the crunchy snow toward the herd of bison. Gunny stopped them when they were still quite far away. "We don't want to get any closer," he warned. "My dad taught me that you always give wild animals plenty of room. You never know what they might do."

"What could that big, fat, shaggy animal do to us?" asked Grant. He thought they looked way too slow to be scary.

"That bison right there can run faster than you can," said Gunny, pointing at the largest animal in the herd. "And if he feels threatened by you, he could charge you and gore you with his horns."

The herd of about 100 brown, wooly bison trudged through the field of white, single file. Many had large, pointy horns, Grant noticed. Christina giggled at their faces—snow and ice clumped and hung from the fur around their noses and mouths.

"It looks like they're having snow for breakfast!" she remarked.

"Actually not," said Gunny, happy that for once he knew more than Molly Jane. "They swing their faces back and forth through the snow to get to the grass beneath."

And sure enough, that's exactly what some of the bison did. Grunting and snuffling, the huge animals pushed their snouts into the snow, shoving it out of the way. Great wads of grass hung out of their mouths as they chomped and chomped until it was gone. Then they started the process again.

"You wanna know something cool about bison?" asked Gunny, as the kids stared at the grazing animals. "Many scientists say that bison are the only mammals that don't suffer from cancer."

"Really?" said Molly Jane. She'd wanted to research about how one mammal could be immune to such a horrible disease that her Aunt Betsy had.

Grant suddenly realized that he could see hundreds of bison all around them near and far. There were large groups and small groups and occasionally a single animal in the miles-long fields, all grazing for the grass hidden under the snow.

"You know, for all the eating these bison do," commented Grant, "I sure haven't seen any bison..."

SPLUNK...

"POOP!!!!!!! AAAAGGGGHHHHH!" Grant shouted.

Because he'd been so busy staring at the animals, Grant had walked straight into a brown, stinky "bison paddy" that had even melted some of the snow around it. He was now stomping around in the snow, trying to shake, rub, and wipe the remnants of the bison's breakfast off his boot and into the snow.

"Oh, Grant!" Christina shrieked. "How does this always happen to you?!"

"Ugh! That smells worse than the mud pots," said Molly Jane, moving downwind.

"Oh, yeah, another cool thing about bison is their poop!" said Gunny, laughing.

"Very funny," said Grant, still stomping, still shaking, still rubbing his boot in a part of the field that had been cleared by bison grazing.

"No, I'm serious," said Gunny. "If you lived in a little house on some prairie way back when, you'd be thrilled to collect lots of fat bison patties to burn for fuel to keep warm or cook with."

Christina gave Gunny a funny look. "Well, maybe not *thrilled*," he added. "Especially since most of the time, it was kids who did the collecting."

"Leave me out of that," grumbled Grant. "I already did my poop part for today."

Grant and Christina wandered toward a group of people dressed in western ponchos and jackets, ornately decorated with Native American symbols and stones. They sat on a large tarp on the edge of the field, sharing food with one another.

"Join us!" One of the women in the group beckoned to the kids. She had a long, dark braid hanging down her back. "We're sharing food that our Shoshone Indian ancestors ate. Try some!"

Hesitantly, Grant and Christina accepted a piece of something that looked like beef jerky.

"This is called *pemmican*—it's bison meat that's been dried, pounded into a powder, then mixed with bison fat," said a man in the group.

"Thank you. Sounds delicious," said Grant sarcastically. He turned to his sister and gave her an "I'll eat it if you'll eat it" look.

They each took a bite, pulling hard to rip a piece of the beef in order to get some in their mouth. As good sports, they chewed and swallowed, with a little bit of effort and forced smiles.

"Wow," continued Grant. "That was very...very...uh..."

"Good," said Christina, finishing her brother's sentence in order to be polite.

"So glad you liked it," said the woman. "It has been curing in its rawhide bag for 30 years to achieve it most authentic taste!"

"Thirty ye–ye–years?" sputtered Grant. He had bison poop on his boot and 30-year-old bison jerky in his belly. So far, this was not one of his best days. The kids thanked the group for their mid-morning snack and headed back toward Gunny and Molly Jane.

"Come on, Christina," urged Grant. "The only way this day can get any better for me is to get back into a little mystery!"

11
CLUES AND CLOUDS

Christina saw Mimi and Papa standing next to a tree intently fiddling with a camera. To her amazement, a bald eagle was perched at the very top of the tree. The bird took off from its perch, swooped down toward the field, and used its talons to pick up a rock squirrel bounding across the snow. It happened so fast it took Christina a second to realize what she had just seen. The eagle took its prey and flew off to the rocky cliffs that bordered the meadow. A distant coyote howl rolled across the rocks.

The bison herd paraded across the road into another part of the park.

"I guess they go wherever they want! It's like they own this place!" said Grant. "That sure would cause a traffic jam if cars were trying to drive down that road!"

"Trust me, it does in the summer at the height of tourist season!" said Molly Jane with a giggle.

A pack of mule deer had moved in and were grazing in the spot the bison cleared earlier. Christina marveled at the amount of wildlife and how active it was, and soooo close!

"Let's look at that clue again," said Gunny, referring to the rock they had found yesterday at Fountain Paint Pots.

Christina pulled the rock out and the kids read the clue:

"That sounds like a pirate and a musician to me," said Grant.

"Really helpful, Grant," said his sister. She looked to Molly Jane for some real help.

Molly Jane had been thinking about the clue since last night. She was still confused by it. She wasn't going to be any help solving the clue this time.

Christina glanced up at the clouds that were now high in the sky over Yellowstone. It felt a lot colder today than it did yesterday with the sun stuck behind the clouds and the wind whipping about. But she didn't give it much thought as they headed off for the next stop in their journey. After all, how could anyone have predicted the treacherous weather that was about to barrel into the park?

12

PANTS PANDEMONIUM

The group had stopped at Sulfur Caldron, just outside Hayden Valley. The water from the springs was splashing and churning a brilliant yellow. Grant watched the bubbling water and held his nose again to block out the stink of the gases. That was when the event they would come to call "Papa's Pants Pandemonium" took place.

Papa sat down on what seemed to be a safe plot of ground—half snowy, half grassy—in order to adjust his snow boots.

"The word caldron comes from the word caldera," explained Mimi to the kids. "And remember, Yellowstone is the world's largest, most active caldera."

As they were moving to another spot to look over the spring, Papa stood up and felt a cold breeze rush past his backside. He turned around and Mimi cried, "The back of Papa's pants is gone!" Papa quickly slapped both hands over his bare backside.

"Mimi! What happened?" Christina yelped.

Quickly unfolding a park trail map and covering Papa's bottom with it, Mimi put the pieces together. "Sulphur Caldron is one of the most acidic springs in all of Yellowstone. The ground all around the springs must be at such a high acid level it can dissolve the pants right off ya!"

Christina would have been embarrassed for her grandfather if Papa, Grant, and Gunny hadn't been laughing their heads off. Soon all six of them were doubled over in fits of laughter and were getting some crazy looks from tourists passing by as they made their way back to the snowmobiles.

Mimi bent over to read the map stuck on Papa to see where they were going next, and all the kids roared once more with laughter.

"No 'butts' about it," Grant said with a giggle, "Papa is showing us the way!"

13

A POINT, A FALLS, AND A CANYON

Mimi and Papa dropped off the kids at Artist Point overlooking the spot where the Lower Falls leads to the Grand Canyon of Yellowstone. Mimi and Papa zoomed off to find a replacement pair of pants. A park guide in a snow coach offered to look out for the kids and take them to the Upper Falls in an hour to reconnect with the grandparents. When Mimi thanked the guide for his assistance, he replied, "You know our motto is, 'If you ever need *anything*, always ask a ranger!' We are here to help!"

Off on their own, the kids stood gazing at one of the most magnificent views in all of Yellowstone.

"I didn't know there were two Grand Canyons in the United States," said Grant, remembering a past escapade with Mimi, Papa, and his sister. "Now I've been to both of them!"

"Well," said Molly Jane, "this Grand Canyon was made because the rhyolite—that's the name of all that rock—was being cut through by the Yellowstone River, not the Colorado River. It may not be as big as the other Grand Canyon, but it is just as beautiful."

Even with the clouds thickening menacingly overhead, the kids made their way up the steep, rocky trail to the top of the falls. The view of the Yellowstone River as it rushed over the Lower Falls was one of the most amazing things Christina had seen since she'd arrived in the world's first national park.

"That's a long way down!" remarked Grant, peering gingerly over the edge of the falls.

The "babysitting" park ranger came alongside the kids when he saw them pointing and motioning all over the place. "You're right," he shouted to be heard over the deafening sound of the rushing water below. "It is a long way down! The Lower Falls is as tall as the Statue of Liberty."

"Whoa!" replied Grant. He thought he could feel the mist from the river hitting him in the face.

Looking past the falls and into the canyon area downstream, Christina could see the sandstone-colored bluffs bordering each side of the river peeking out from the snow. The bluffs gave way to rocky cliffs higher above. Occasionally, a grove of trees draped in icicles clung precariously to the steep slopes. The colors of these rocks must be why this place is called YELLOW-stone, she thought.

"Maybe Mimi and Papa will let us hike to the bottom of this canyon," said Grant hopefully. "Maybe we could go fishing in the river."

"I'm not going down there with you," said Gunny. "My great-great-grandfather..."

"You mean the one with the treasure?" whispered Grant, so the ranger couldn't hear.

"Yeah, that one," continued Gunny. "In his journals, he wrote that hiking to the bottom of the Grand Canyon of Yellowstone was like hiking 5 miles in, but felt like hiking 35 miles out!"

"Fishing would be fun, if you got down there," added the ranger. "The Cutthroat and Rainbow trout would be a great catch for you and your grandpa."

Grant and Gunny spun around so fast the ranger had to take a step back.

"Those are names of fish?" asked Grant. "Fish that live in this river?"

"Sure are," replied the ranger.

The ranger headed down the trail leading back to Artist Point. "Meet me at the snow coach when you guys are ready," he called.

The four kids began to search in earnest for the symbol they had seen twice before. They had no luck at the top of the falls. Back at the Artist Point overlook, Gunny and Grant spied the outline of a fish carved into the side of the walkway. Next to the carving were two words. It had to be the clue!

Excited, but puzzled, Christina, Grant, Gunny, and Molly Jane headed to the snow coach, too. The "babysitting ranger" was having a powwow with another ranger. Their backs were to the kids, but they must have heard the kids coming their way. The two men quickly hushed and turned around to open the doors of the coach.

"Oh, great!" Christina muttered.

"It's about time," said their babysitter. "Ranger Magnus here wanted to be sure you kids were staying out of trouble."

Ranger Magnus looked at the kids as if they were ruining his day. "I'll ride with you to meet your grandparents," he said.

The kids climbed into the "van on skis" and got settled.

"Great," said Christina, giving a worried look to Grant and the others. "That's soooo nice of you. NOT!" she whispered under her breath.

14
WHOLE LOT OF SHAKING GOING ON

At the picnic area by Upper Falls, Grant inhaled his peanut butter and banana sandwich. Not only had Mimi gotten Papa new snow pants, she'd also bought box lunches for everyone.

"Thank goodness we aren't eating pemmican again," Grant said.

"Aw, come on, Grant!" Christina said, laughing. Secretly she was glad, too, because she still had its awful taste in her mouth.

"Will someone tell me what we are going to do about Ranger Magnus?" asked Gunny. He didn't want that creep to come between him and the family treasure they were hopefully close to finding.

"I think we just ignore him and continue to be the fun-loving, sightseeing kids that we have been," said Christina. "We don't want to draw any attention to ourselves."

"But he is paying attention to us," said Molly Jane. "He turns up all over the place."

"I'll ask Papa about him. Sometimes..." started Christina. "Oh...oh...whoa!!!!"

Before she could finish her sentence, the picnic table and the kids began to rattle and shake. "What's going on?!" she cried, grabbing hold of the side of the table so she wouldn't fall to the ground.

"Yiiiiikes!" screamed Grant. He threw his arms around Gunny and together they rumbled and bumbled up and down on the picnic bench.

"Iiiitttt'sss aaaannnn eeeaaarrtthh qquuuakkke!" cried Molly Jane. Her glasses bounced right off her face.

Just as soon as it started, it was over.

Mimi and Papa ran over to see if the kids were ok.

"Whew!" said Grant, letting go of Gunny. He patted his friend on the back.

"How 'bout them apples?" said Papa, smiling. "That's the strongest quake I've ever felt in this park."

"Do you mean you've felt other earthquakes at Yellowstone, Papa?" asked Christina. "When?"

"*Every time* I've ever come here," replied Papa. "You don't realize it, but there have probably been earthquakes happening since you've been here, too."

"But I haven't felt anything before this," Christina said.

"There are tiny tremors occurring all the time, cowgirl," he continued. "Often as many as 2,000 a year! Sometimes you can feel them; sometimes you can't. But that's the nature of the caldera and the magma chamber that created Yellowstone. It's moving and changing all the time, and the earth's surface moves and changes along with it."

"Mimi, it's too bad you didn't get us some ice cream and milk for lunch," said Grant to his grandmother, who was rubbing Christina's back to calm her.

"Why in the world would I have done that, Grant?" Mimi asked.

"Because we could have had MILKSHAKES!" squealed Grant, delighted with his joke.

"No matter what happens, Grant can always make it be about food!" said his sister, laughing.

They gathered up their trash, being extra careful to leave the park as nice as they found it. As they headed to Tower Falls, Gunny felt relief that they had found that last clue but was worried they could have another visit from Ranger Magnus!

15
PETRIFIED AND MORE PETRIFIED!

While the kids took in the view of the black volcanic spires of Tower Fall, snow began to fall lightly from the grey clouds. It was just as well that the trail to the base of the fall was closed. The switchback path would have been as slippery as a ski slope, and not safe for traveling.

The snow was falling a little harder when they got to the Petrified Tree. The tree was, in fact, only part of a tree jutting out from the ground. It looked like it had been snapped in half at the center, the top nowhere to be found.

"What's the big deal about a tree stump?" questioned Grant.

"This is no regular tree stump," said Molly Jane, leaning against the fence, which protected the tree from park visitors. "This was a redwood tree that lived almost 50 million years ago. When the Yellowstone volcanoes erupted, the ash buried the trees so quickly that it preserved them instead of destroying them."

"I've seen tiny petrified fossils in my science class," said Christina, wiping snowflakes from her video camera lens. "This is an enormous fossil!"

Through the falling snow, the kids could see the remains of the other two petrified trees that used to be in the same area before previous park visitors removed them piece by piece, thoughtlessly taking the pieces home as souvenirs. No wonder there is a fence around it now, thought Christina.

In the forested area to the left of where they were standing, there was a rustling in the trees and the crunch of snowpack. Grant absentmindedly wandered closer to see what was making the sound. The crunching in the snow got louder and a tree shook gently.

Appearing out of nowhere, Grant spied an enormous bear lumbering through the forest. It was snorting and blowing air in and out of its nose in a puff of white vapor.

"Hey, bear," whispered Grant, his voice filled with surprise. He stood as still as the tree nearby. And, as petrified.

The bear padded forward a few feet and then stopped to dig in the snow. Grant figured the bear was looking for food. He hoped that young boys were not on the bear's menu today.

"Hey, bear," Grant whispered again, and now his knees were shaking a little bit.

Slowly and quietly, Papa came to stand next to Grant. Each of them stared at the bear as it hunted for food, making popping sounds with its teeth.

"Papa?" said Grant, barely above a whisper. "Is that a grizzly bear?"

"I don't know, Grant," answered Papa, speaking just as quietly. "It might be a black bear."

"What's the difference?" asked Grant, not really knowing why it mattered.

"Well," said Papa, pointing to a nearby tree, "why don't you go climb that tree right there? If the bear climbs up after you, it's a black bear. If the bear knocks the tree over, it's a griz."

Grant shot his grandfather a silent glare that was met with a broad smile. Snow was falling steadily and sounds of faraway waterfalls and bird calls and coyote howls filled the air.

Just as Grant wondered when and how they were going to get back to their family and friends, the most unlikely thing happened. Papa and Grant found themselves not only in the company of an oversized maybe black/maybe grizzly bear, but also an approaching young bull moose. It was as tall as two Papas and must have weighed as much as a small car. Grant could tell that neither animal had yet caught the scent of the other. Each concentrated on their current meal.

Papa's smile faded to a look of concern. "Grant, don't move a muscle," he whispered as his eyes shifted from side to side, looking for a place where he could take his grandson to safety should either animal run in their direction.

The grazing moose stepped on a dead tree limb on the ground and it snapped in half like a toothpick. That sound made the bear flinch and turn quickly in the direction of the moose.

The moose saw the bear move and bolted through the trees away from Papa and Grant. The bear gave a quick chase but stopped without ever really challenging the moose. Luckily, the bear had run far enough that grandfather and grandson could quickly move out of the trees and back to the snowmobiles where Mimi, Christina, Gunny, and Molly Jane were waiting.

"There you are! Where have you two been?" asked Mimi, relieved.

"Didn't you want to look at the petrified tree?" asked Christina.

Papa chuckled and put his arm around Grant's shoulder. Grant's heart still felt like it was beating like a war drum.

"We saw it," said Papa. "And that wasn't the only petrifying thing we saw!"

16
MENACING MINERVA

The kids were happy to be off on their own on the boardwalks and trails around Mammoth Hot Springs. Papa was refueling the snowmobiles and Mimi was sipping hot cider and warming by the fire at the Mammoth Hotel.

"Everything in this park is ancient," Gunny said, frustrated. He was repeating the last clue over and over in his mind.

"We've got to figure this out," said Christina. "If it snows any harder, Mimi and Papa will make us go back to the hotel."

Snow was accumulating on the trail they were walking on, but it was not sticking to the rocks that were stair-stepping down the hillside. The familiar mist of the hot springs was everywhere.

"Is that waterfall frozen?" asked Grant, pointing toward the springs. "I thought the water coming out of the hot springs was HOT. How could it freeze?"

"It's actually not water at all, Grant," said Molly Jane, cleaning snow off her glasses for like the millionth time. "Those are mineral deposits called travertine. Here, the water heated by the magma below seeps up through the limestone rock that is in this part of Yellowstone."

Christina pulled out her camera to zoom in on Minerva Terrace's perfectly sculpted travertine steps.

Molly Jane continued, "It's kind of a complex scientific explanation that I don't totally understand, but somehow the combination of heat, water, limestone, and air creates these travertine deposits that are forming even while we're watching them."

"So, not everything in this park is old, after all," said Christina.

"Well then, the treasure must not be here," said Grant. "We can take a break from mystery-solving for a while," he added, shuffling through the snow down the boardwalk. "And that suits me fine. It's been a crazy day—even for me!"

As Christina and Gunny walked around the domed hot spring cone known as Liberty Cap, they mulled over the latest clue and his great-great-grandfather's treasure. Christina really wanted to help him find it. She just hoped HER grandparents and the worsening weather wouldn't interfere with their searching.

Gunny touched Christina lightly on the shoulder and pointed down the walkway. "Look, it's Magnus," he said. "And he is headed right for us."

Ranger Magnus glared down the boardwalk with a sinister stare, and stamped along more quickly when he spied the kids.

Christina glanced around quickly for Grant and Molly Jane, who had just been handed a camera to take a group picture of some tourists from Australia.

"Say 'Moose Muffins'!" urged Grant, coaxing a smile out of the tourists. Molly Jane snapped the picture and handed the camera back to a member of the group.

Christina and Gunny high-stepped it over to Grant and Molly Jane. "Come on!" Christina said to them both. "It's time to head back to Minerva Terrace."

The four children skidded along as fast as they could on the slippery snow, but Magnus was closing in on them. "Hey! You kids!" bellowed the park ranger. "You better stop right now!"

The kids sprinted down the boardwalk and onto the trail back to Minerva Terrace. They caught a lucky break when Magnus slipped on an icy patch on the walkway and face-planted right into some freshly fallen snow.

"We need to get to the parking area!" shouted Christina to the others. "Papa will be waiting for us and Magnus won't bother us with Papa there."

But their luck did not hold out. Two more oversized, unfriendly looking park officials appeared in front of them on the trail. The kids stopped in their tracks and turned to look for another way to run. But there was Magnus right behind them.

They were TRAPPED like rats in a maze!

Magnus had recovered from his fall but he looked MAD! His face was red, his coat sleeve was ripped, and snow was clotted in his hair and bushy eyebrows.

"You kids need to come with us," he growled. "Right now!"

17
FEARSOME FORT?

Christina's thoughts were almost drowned out by the noise of the treads moving the snow coach down the trail. What did Magnus want from them? And why didn't she bring the cell phone that Mimi always made her carry when they were on trips like this? One phone call to her protective grandparents could fix this whole situation. Seeing a ghost at Old Faithful Inn was better than this mess!

After stopping to allow a herd of bison to nonchalantly mosey across the road, the snow coach drove into what looked like a small village of older, but official-looking stone and wooden buildings. Grant noticed a sign that said: FORT YELLOWSTONE.

"We're at a military fort!" Grant exclaimed, with a look of fear. "They're going to throw us in the stockade!"

"No, they aren't," Christina said, trying to act unafraid.

Molly Jane wanted a new experience at Yellowstone, but this was not it. "What have we gotten ourselves into?" she asked the other kids, to no response.

The wind and the snow whipped around the buildings and the trees. Christina spied two elk, with long pointy antlers, strolling past the front of one of the buildings. Snow was gathering on their heads and backs, and even in the nooks and crannies of their antlers.

The snow coach skidded to a stop in front of a tan building with a front porch. Though nearly covered in snow, Christina could tell it had a red roof. Her heart leaped with joy when she saw a man in a black cowboy hat and a woman in a coat and hat as red as the roof of the building. It was Mimi and Papa!

She and Grant scrambled out of the vehicle and into the waiting arms of their grandparents.

"Thanks for bringing the kids to us," Papa said to Ranger Magnus. "It gave the little lady and myself some extra time by the warm fire!"

"Our pleasure," said Magnus, looking a bit annoyed. He gave the kids one more stern look and started to say something, but instead turned and hopped back aboard the snow coach. Grant waved to him with a smirk as they drove away.

"Ok, kids," said Mimi. "We are dropping Gunny and Molly Jane off at the visitor's center to meet their folks. Then we are headed back to the Old Faithful Snow Lodge."

"And we gotta move fast," said Papa. "There's a doozy of a storm moving in and we want to be safe and sound in our beds when it hits."

18
GEEZER GEYSER!

Grant grabbed the jumbo marshmallow that was floating in his hot chocolate and stuffed it into his mouth. "Hey, Christina! How do I look?" he said, and gave Christina a grin smothered in gooey white fluff.

"Gross!" squealed Christina. I guess that's what little brothers are for, she thought, sipping her hot chocolate like the young lady Mimi expected her to be.

The family made it to the Old Faithful Snow Lodge just in time for the storm to barrel full force into Yellowstone. Outside, the wind howled louder than any coyote ever could. After dinner, Mimi went up to the suite to write, while Papa visited with other guests by the stone fireplace.

Grant and Christina sat at one of the rustic wooden desks placed throughout the Lodge, finishing their hot chocolate. Grant flipped through a pamphlet and guidebook.

"What are you looking at?" asked Christina.

"I dunno," answered Grant. "I guess it's information about Old Faithful."

Christina knew that Old Faithful was the most popular place for tourists to visit at Yellowstone. They had seen the geyser erupt, on their way out to sightsee this morning. But they were in such a hurry to get to Hayden Valley that they didn't stop to admire it. Besides, Mimi said there was going to be a special gathering around the geyser tomorrow night around midnight. It was a special "Full Moon Celebration," and Mimi and Papa had been invited to attend. Mimi said that would be the time they could enjoy Yellowstone's most beloved attraction.

Looking out the window at the storm, Christina could only wonder if such an outdoor celebration would take place. She had never seen such a blizzard!

"Look at this!" urged Grant, pushing the pamphlet at his sister.

Christina read:

Old Faithful isn't the biggest geyser in the park or even the most spectacular. But it attracts big crowds because its eruptions are generally predictable. Old Faithful sends a plume of hot water skyward in intervals ranging between 33 minutes and 120 minutes, though the majority of eruptions occur every 70 minutes or so. This is especially impressive since scientists believe that Old Faithful has been active for 25,000 years.

Christina looked at her brother. He was smiling at her, thankfully without a marshmallow stuck in his teeth this time. She grinned as soon as she realized why Grant was smiling.

"Old Faithful is ancient!" said Grant, proud of himself for putting the pieces of the clue together. "I mean, 25,000 years is OLD!" "And it's loyal to the park visitors because its eruptions are predictable!" said Christina. "It's FAITHFUL! The clue points to Old Faithful!"

"That's gotta mean Gunny's treasure is out there—out at Old Faithful!" said Grant.

The smile left Christina's face. "Actually, that isn't such good news," she said in a sad voice.

"Sure it is!" said Grant. "We figured out the clue and it leads right here next to us—right outside the lodge!"

"Yeah, but it also means that Gunny's treasure is being covered up with a ton of snow from this storm," said Christina. "There's no way we'll ever find it!"

19

CLUELESS TREASURE

The kids had played cards—Go Fish and Hearts—trying to pass the time until they could get back outside to explore the park with their grandparents, but more importantly, look for that treasure.

Last night's storm had dropped 11 inches of snow on Yellowstone National Park, with snow drifts as high as a two-story building in some places. Papa said they had to wait until the park service had plowed some of the roads and trails before they would go back out. Every five minutes they chimed, "Is it time yet?"

The grandparents finally gave in at lunchtime and they headed out in the freshly fallen snow. The first stop of their final day in the park was Norris Geyser Basin. The boardwalks and trails were smothered with several inches of snow, which made it more challenging to walk around, but it didn't stop Christina and Grant. They raced ahead of Mimi and Papa, who were moving more slowly, crunching and wading through the snowpack.

Steam from the geysers, vents, and hot springs was thick around them, spiraling toward the clear blue sky that had reappeared after the storm.

"This says that this is the tallest active geyser!" screamed Christina to Grant, pointing at a sign.

"What?!" Grant screamed back. He couldn't hear his sister. They were standing in front of Steamboat Geyser as it erupted and spewed water and steam 40 feet into the air.

Christina shook her head at her brother and crunched through the snow down the trail.

Grant caught up to her saying, "Did you know that was the world's tallest, active geyser that we just saw?"

Christina laughed. "Really?!" she said with sarcasm. "That's fascinating!"

The kids were enjoying their day in the snow at Yellowstone. They looked forward to meeting Gunny and Molly Jane back at the Old Faithful Snow Lodge later that night. Mimi and Papa had invited both families to join them for the Full Moon Celebration. They couldn't wait to talk to their new friends about the clue and then go hunting for Gunny's treasure that just had to be there somewhere—even if it was buried under all that snow.

They circled the lower trail of Norris Basin and worked their way back up toward the entrance. They promised Mimi and Papa they would meet them in the bookstore across from the museum.

"I haven't used my video camera enough," said Christina, pulling it out of her coat pocket.

"Well, ok. Let's film here—Minute Geyser!" suggested Grant. "It erupts every minute. And while we wait for a minute to pass, you can film me making a snow angel!"

Grant flopped back into the snow and began waving his arms and legs up and down and back and forth. Getting up and brushing the snow from his backside and head, he said, "Not bad if I do say so myself!"

Christina turned the lens of the camera from Grant's snow angel to Minute Geyser, awaiting its eruption. Nothing happened.

"Ok," said Grant. "One more snow angel!" And he again flopped into the snow, arms and legs flailing.

Again, Christina focused on the second snow angel and then up to Minute Geyser. Still nothing.

"You'll have to make an awful lot of snow angels before this geyser will erupt again," said a lady, walking up to the two children.

"But it says it erupts every minute," said Grant, pointing to the sign.

"Ah, but if you read more carefully, it says it USED to erupt every minute," the lady continued. "The land and the features of Yellowstone are a gift to its visitors. But sometimes the visitors are destructive to its beauty."

Grant looked puzzled and Christina turned to continue filming the dormant geyser.

"Minute Geyser no longer erupts because over the years, visitors carelessly threw so many rocks into the geyser that it has clogged up the vent," the lady said. "I guess each person said to themselves, 'What's the harm with ONE rock?'"

"If hundreds and thousands of people throw just ONE rock, that's a lot of rocks," said Christina.

"The same kind of thing happened at Blue Star Pool on Geyser Hill," the lady said, standing alongside Christina. "A park worker set out to remove pennies that people had thrown into it over the years. They hoped to unclog the vent so the pool's temperature would increase and its beautiful blue colors would be restored."

"And?" asked Grant.

"And, in the first 15 minutes of work, he removed 700 pennies," the lady said.

"Seven hundred?!" said Grant. "Man, I could do something a lot better with seven dollars than clog up a hot spring." He was thinking of baseball cards and action figures.

"Then be sure you tell your friends and family that to maintain the treasure of a national park, they must treat it as a treasure," finished the lady, and she headed down the snowy trail.

Christina turned off her video camera and put it back in her pocket. "Come on, Grant," she said. "Let's get to the bookstore and find Mimi and Papa. That lady made me realize I might know just where Gunny's hidden treasure is!"

20

EYEBALL GLORY

In 1950, park workers pulled out more than $100 in change, along with logs, tin cans, towels, and even a pair of underwear from Morning Glory Pool. That's what Christina and Grant learned that afternoon while they explored the geyser basin near Old Faithful. Mimi and Papa were pleased the kids learned that in order for people to continue to enjoy the breathtaking beauty of Yellowstone, they must be respectful of its features.

The deep blue and neon green center of Morning Glory pool was encircled by the familiar mustard yellows and browns that were typical of the scalding hot pools. Christina could see why it was one of the most photographed and painted spots in all of Yellowstone. Grant liked it for a completely different reason.

"It looks like an oversized eyeball!" he cried.

Gunny, Molly Jane, and their families were waiting for Mimi, Papa, and the kids at the snow lodge when they arrived back from their last afternoon of sightseeing. After a delicious dinner of bison chili and sourdough biscuits, the adults retired to their usual comfy spots around the enormous fireplace.

Meanwhile, the kids headed upstairs to find a great mystery hunters meeting spot among the knotty wooden rails of the third floor balcony.

"I can't believe the clue led right to Old Faithful," said Gunny excitedly.

"Gosh, I sure hope the ghost of the Old Faithful Inn hasn't found it first," teased Grant.

Molly Jane's eyes got wide. "Ghost?"

"It's a long story! Anyway, I don't think we have to worry about Mr. Reamer's ghost tonight," assured Christina. "We need to get outside to the geyser so we can start searching."

The adults gave permission for them to go outside as long as they promised to stay near the lodge, and of course they promised. Christina hoped Mimi and Papa couldn't see her fingers crossed behind her back.

As they neared the Old Faithful viewing area, the kids split up to search for another symbol or any spot that looked like a good place to hide a treasure. The moon was as round and silvery as a pie tin and its light reflected off the powder-white snow like a Hollywood searchlight. Snow crunched beneath their boots like cereal. The winter night's air stung their cheeks. Eyelashes grew frosty. Stars glittered like Mimi's party diamond jewelry.

Grant and Christina *crunched crunched crunched* to the area just to the north of the benches that encircled the geyser. They continued out through the field and toward some trees near Firehole River. They could hear the river's throaty gurgle in front of them and a coyote howling morosely in the distance.

Suddenly, Old Faithful erupted behind them in an early *whoosh*, then a growing, almost squealing skybound stream. Grant and Christina spun around to see it in the light of the moon. The next time it erupts will be during the Full Moon celebration, thought Christina.

"Let's hurry, Grant," she urged. "We don't have much time left before Mimi and Papa come outside. That would be the end of our treasure hunting."

Grant scanned the ground, the trees, and the rocks. He gasped, "Look! I can't believe it!"

"Did you find it? Did you find the treasure?" asked Christina, running over.

"No, but look at what I did find!" he said. Grant bent down in the snow and pulled up a set of antlers a moose had shed sometime during the winter. The points were sticking out in all directions and he had to use extra oomph to hold it up. "Look, Christina! Antlers!"

"That's great, little brother, really it is," she said. "But please help me search. We're running out of time."

While Grant investigated the antlers a little more, Christina spied a patch of land bordered by a large boulder and four tall trees. It looked like a small camp area. A wooden sign nailed to one of the trees said:

It makes sense, thought Christina. This site would be the perfect place for a weary

For those who hike through nature's treasure, marvel and rest here at your leisure.

hiker to stop, rest, and appreciate nature's impressive thermal display all around him. Yellowstone National Park was really a treasure all by itself.

At the base of the tree was a mound of snow. When Christina spied it, she ran ahead and with her hands, dug hard and fast, her fingers tingling with frostbite. After she'd scraped the snow level, she expected to find dirt, but instead felt a canvas fabric. A camp pack! Could this hold the treasure Gunny's great-great-grandfather left before he died?

She shifted in the snow so the moonlight could shine on the ground by the base of the tree. Quickly she dug around the canvas with a stick, and with two hard pulls, popped it out of the ground and into her hands.

"Grant! Grant!" she shouted, turning around to run to show her brother. "I found it! I found the..."

What Christina found was that she was face-to-face with a black bear.

21

MOOSE MAN SAVES THE DAY!

Grant heard his sister calling. He knew he needed to get back to the search. He propped the antlers by a nearby tree. Later, he would ask Papa if he could keep them, though he wasn't sure how they would fit on the *Mystery Girl*.

Grant headed in the direction he saw Christina walk a few minutes ago. When he caught up, he saw her holding a canvas bag and standing very still, staring at something. "What is it, Christina?" he called. "What did you find?"

Christina did not take her eyes off the bear. She nodded her head ever so gently and, since she was holding the camp pack in her right hand, she slightly raised her left index finger to point in the direction of the bear.

Grant's eyes darted from his sister to where she was pointing. There was a bear, smaller than the bear he and Papa saw yesterday, but a bear nonetheless. It was sitting on its back legs, front paws in the air, staring right at Christina.

"Ok, don't move," instructed Grant, trying to sound like Papa.

"What are we going to do?" asked Christina, in a whimper. "Maybe you should go get Papa."

"Umm, no. No," said Grant. "I think I might have a plan."

Grant very slowly walked backwards to where he left the moose antlers. He reached down and picked them up and waded through the snow until he was standing behind the bear—far behind the bear.

He glanced over toward the boulder and then toward the trees. Finally, he gave his sister a reassuring look.

"Hey, bear!" Grant shouted. "You want a moose muffin?" He hiked the antlers over his head and began stomping around, snow flying every which way.

The bear spun his head around in surprise and dropped down on all fours. Curious about this odd-looking moose, he lumbered toward Grant. Grant and his antlers went running toward the boulder with the bear running behind him. He ran around the backside of the enormous rock, made a sharp right turn, and flung the moose antlers out into the snow.

As Grant had hoped, the bear followed the antlers. Grant ran straight to Christina, grabbed her hand, and they sprinted as fast as they could back toward the Old Faithful geyser.

Gunny and Molly Jane ran over to meet Grant and Christina, who were sitting on a log bench on a viewing platform. They were as pale as the snow and breathing heavily. Beads of sweat dotted their foreheads, which seemed strange on this cold night.

"What happened to you guys?" asked Molly Jane.

"Don't ask!" said Christina. She clutched her brother's hand.

"Christina, show Gunny what you found," said Grant, officially changing the subject.

Christina held up an old, dirty, wet camp pack.

"Could that be my great-great-grandfather's camp pack?" asked Gunny. "Where did you find it?"

"Oh, just out in the WILD!" said Christina.

Gunny took the canvas bag and was just about to open it when Ranger Magnus came walking toward them.

"I see you found the hiker's treasure," he said in a low voice. "Perhaps you should give that bag to me."

22
SAFETY POINTS?

The kids' grim faces were relieved when Mimi, Papa, Mr. Mitchell, and the Edwards walked up right behind Ranger Magnus.

Gunny quickly opened the camp pack to find a gold compass inside. It was old and worn—obviously well-used over the years. He turned it left and right and watched the arrow as it spun from north to south and back again.

"You kids have found something special, haven't you?" said Mr. Mitchell. "That compass was my great grandfather James' compass. He used it on all of his hiking expeditions back in his day."

"How did you know what we had, Dad?" asked Gunny.

"Ranger Magnus told us he thought you children might be searching for that lost compass," said Papa. "He saw you looking at great grandfather James' map back at Yellowstone Lake two days ago."

"I recognized the symbol that was at the top of the map," said Ranger Magnus. For the first time, the kids thought his voice sounded kind. "It had to be the map that would lead to the compass. Hikers and park visitors have been searching for it for years."

"Why?" asked Grant. "Does the gold make it worth a lot of money?"

"No. It's not valuable because of money," said Magnus. "It's valuable because of its history."

"Gunny, we are going to donate the compass to Yellowstone Park to display in their Park Ranger museum," said Mr. Mitchell.

"If you only wanted a compass for the museum," began Christina, "then why have you been chasing us around the park?"

"I wanted to check on you kids," replied the ranger. "This park can be a dangerous place. I was worried you might find yourselves in a scary situation if you were truly searching for the compass."

"Ranger Magnus, thank you so much for your help and concern," said Mimi, smiling through her sparkly glasses. "I assure you these children have taken every precaution to be safe around this park. Right, kids?"

"Right, Mimi!" said Grant and Christina, together, fingers crossed behind their backs. They smiled as they glanced over to the snowy woods where their bear might still be chasing the phantom moose!

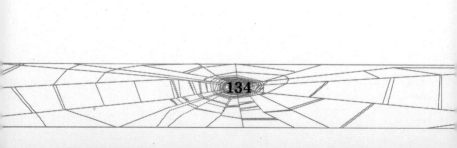

23
MOONLIGHT MERRIMENT

As the full moon rose higher in the night sky, a bonfire blazed and a band sent the sounds of banjo and harmonica out into the forest. The Full Moon Celebration was in full swing and everyone was enjoying the festivities!

Papa tapped the toe of his cowboy boot to the western music. Mimi smiled when Grant handed her a fresh mug of steaming hot chocolate. "Toss in a few more marshmallows, Grant!" Mimi told him.

Grant gave Mimi two marshmallows and stuck two on a roasting stick. He plopped down next to Christina and plunged his stick over the campfire next to hers.

"I'm going to burn mine to a crisp," said Grant. "The blacker the better!"

"It figures," said Christina, knocking him with her shoulder.

Molly Jane walked over and sat down. "You'll never guess what my parents just told me," she said. "We're coming to Yellowstone AGAIN in the spring. They want to see all the baby bison that will be born by then."

"Wow, your parents really do love this place," said Grant. "I think you could say they 'treasure' it!"

"Well, I treasure it, too," said Christina. "It is amazing what geological magnificence can be created by volcanoes, magma, and fire."

"You mean wonderful things like my burned-up marshmallows?" asked Grant, pulling two charred, black briquettes out of the bonfire.

"Yeah, just like your marshmallows!" said Christina.

Grant shoved the burned marshmallows into his mouth, chewing the ooey-gooey mess and licking his fingers one by one.

It was just before midnight and the kids turned to look as Old Faithful erupted into the night sky. The water and the steam glistened in the moonlight. Christina felt thankful that she got to experience Yellowstone and its national treasures with Grant and Mimi and Papa.

She turned to her grandmother to say thank you for bringing her on the trip, but before she could say anything, Mimi spoke first.

"Christina, Grant! Look at me!" squealed Mimi, flashing them a gloppy, white marshmallow smile.

All the kids laughed. They loved to see the adults have fun, too. Besides, thought Christina, maybe that would make Mimi and Papa be in such a good mood that they might bring them back to Yellowstone in the spring, too.

She decided to ask them in the morning, but first, Old Faithful was commanding their attention. Water shooting skyward, hissing steam spewing into the crisp night air—it was an extraordinary, volcano-induced finale to their mysterious trip. Oh, what a sight!

The End

 Disclaimer:

 Many actions in this book are fictional.

 Due to recent policy changes...

...all Yellowstone National Park snowmobilers must be accompanied by a guide.

<u>Yellowstone</u>
<u>by Christina</u>

Dear Emily,

Well, we just had the trip of a lifetime! Yellowstone National Park is AWESOME! I can honestly now say that I have seen, heard, smelled, tasted, and felt GEOLOGY! I have walked among wildlife (and Grant even stepped in their poop!) and learned so much. Grant wants to grow up and be a park ranger. Mimi will probably write a mystery about this place! And Papa took a gazillion pictures. We sure are lucky that we have a National Park system and that one of those is Yellowstone! Well, that's all for now. See you soon, back at school. Remind me and I'll tell you about Robert Reamer's ghost!"

Your BFF,
Christina

Now...go to

www.carolemarshmysteries.com
and...

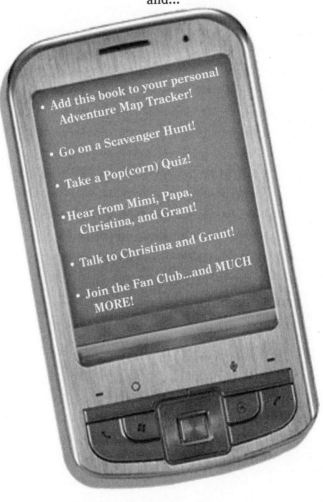

- Add this book to your personal Adventure Map Tracker!

- Go on a Scavenger Hunt!

- Take a Pop(corn) Quiz!

- Hear from Mimi, Papa, Christina, and Grant!

- Talk to Christina and Grant!

- Join the Fan Club...and MUCH MORE!

GLOSSARY

caldera: a sunken area left by a volcanic eruption

fumarole: a hole, or steam vent, near a volcano where smoke comes out

geyser: a hot spring that shoots water into the air

hot spot: a place where magma rises close to the surface of the land and threatens to erupt

mudpots: bubbling hot mud holes near volcanoes

travertine: a form of limestone rock made by hot springs

SAT GLOSSARY

tolerate: to accept or allow

specialize: to learn to do a specific task or job very well

menace: to threaten

simultaneous: when two or more things happen at the same time

continuous: without stopping

Enjoy this exciting excerpt from:

THE MYSTERY

ON THE

Oregon
Trail

1
GATEWAY TO THE WEST

Grant squished his face against the rectangular glass window and squinted. He shoved his messy blond hair away from his eyes.

"I think I can see Independence from here!" he said. He whirled around to have Mimi look and bumped right into Christina.

"OUCH!" Christina cried. "Um, that was my foot."

"Sorry, but I think I can see Independence from here," Grant insisted. "Look!"

Christina glared out the window, squinting her eyes against the sunlight.

"Nope, I don't think so. Independence is too far away," she said.

"But I know that's..." Grant argued.

"We'll be there soon enough," Mimi interrupted. "You two just enjoy the view. It's spectacular! They say you can see for 30 miles on a clear day like today!"

Grant and Christina couldn't argue with their grandmother because the view was amazing. They were standing 630 feet in the air at the top of the Gateway Arch in St. Louis, Missouri—the official start of the Oregon Trail. Grant felt like he was on top of the world!

"Did you know," Mimi began, "that the Gateway Arch is twice as tall as the Statue of Liberty and the tallest national monument in the United States?"

Grant shook his head silently, still mesmerized by the view. Christina watched the people below moving around like tiny floating toys. Her eyes scanned the flat western land she'd soon be traveling—not by car or bus or train—but by covered wagon!

"The view may be spectacular," said Papa in his booming voice, "but it sure is high up here."

"Come on, Papa," said Christina, "you're the cowboy pilot! You fly the *Mystery Girl* all over the world. You can't be afraid of heights!"

"Well, I'm in control of the Mystery Girl when I fly," Papa explained. "This arch is entirely different!"

Grant and Christina giggled at Papa's anxious expression. It was funny, and rare, to see him nervous in his big cowboy hat and tough leather boots. Grant and Christina knew their grandparents well and often traveled with them. Mimi was a children's mystery book writer, and Papa flew her anywhere she needed to go in his red-and-white plane, the *Mystery Girl*.

Suddenly, the tour guide chimed in on the intercom. "Thank you for visiting the Gateway Arch, America's Gateway to the West!"

That was their cue to make room for the next group of eager tourists. Grant and Christina gladly made their way to the tram that would take them on the steep return ride to the ground.

"Here we go again—the worst part of the whole trip," Papa grumbled. The ride to the top of the arch had not gone so well for Papa and Mimi. The family was crammed together in a little egg-shaped pod that zoomed up the inside of the arch. Mimi felt a bit faint and Papa's face was a bright shade of fire-truck red the entire time.

"What do you mean, Papa?" Grant asked. "The ride up to the top was the best part!" He grinned at Christina, who was also looking forward to the rollercoaster ride back down the arch.

"Yeah," Christina said, "maybe we'll get stuck!"

"Stuck?" Mimi asked, alarmed.

"Before we got here," Christina explained, "I read online that just a couple of years ago, the power went out in the tram. People were stuck in the thing for hours!"

"And that makes you excited?" Mimi asked, creasing her eyebrows in a frown.

"Oh, Mimi, it would be an adventure!" said Grant with a mischievous smile. "You love adventures!"

"Not that kind of adventure!" Mimi replied, almost shouting.

"No, sir-eee," Papa drawled. "An adventure like that is more of a BADventure!"

Grant and Christina giggled as their uneasy grandparents stepped into their tram car. Before the doors shut, Grant took one last look out the rectangular windows lining the inside of the arch.

"The Wild West! I can't wait!" he exclaimed. "Yee Haw!"

2
HOME ON THE RANGE

Christina slowly opened her eyes. Her long, shiny, brown hair stuck to her face with sweat. The sun blared down in the backseat of Mimi and Papa's rental car. Their drive from St. Louis to Independence, Missouri took longer than she expected and she must have dozed off. The last time she looked out the window, the scenery consisted of skyscrapers, rivers, and highways. Now, she saw nothing but flat land, grass, and dust—lots of dust!

Christina glanced at the seat next to her where Grant was busy clicking away on his video game. Christina nudged his side with her elbow.

"Hey, Grant, have you seen where we are?" she asked.

"Yeah, it's the prairie, duh!" Grant said, never taking his bright blue eyes off the video game screen. "You've been asleep forever!"

"It's a good thing you got some sleep, Christina," Papa said from the front seat. "We've got a lot of work ahead of us."

"Speaking of work," said Mimi, "there's the sign for Independence city limits right there!"

Christina watched the sign whoosh by and fade away as they sped down the highway.

"What is *that*?" Grant asked, pointing off to the side of the road at a long line of giant, white arches covering boxy, wooden wagons. In the front of each wagon were two horses attached with harnesses. They kicked at the dusty ground with their rough hooves and whinnied across the quiet prairie.

"That's a train of prairie schooners," said Mimi.

"Prairie whats?" Grant asked, confused.

"Schooners," Mimi replied. *"Prairie*

Schooner was the nickname given to covered wagons..."

"I know why, Mimi!" Christina said, interrupting Mimi in the middle of her sentence.

"Alright, why?" Mimi asked, adjusting the sparkly red sunglasses perched on her nose.

"Because the white wagon tops look like sails from boats floating across the prairie," Christina explained.

"You're absolutely correct," Mimi said with a big smile. "Someone's done their research on the Oregon Trail!"

Christina glanced at Grant with raised eyebrows. He frowned.

"Well, I don't need to do research," Grant said, "I know how to be a real cowboy just like Papa. It comes natural!"

Papa nodded at Grant in the rear view mirror and grinned as he pulled the car to a stop. Grant and Christina jumped out of the car and raced toward the wagons.

"Whoa! Look at those wheels!" said Grant.

"Yeah, they're huge!" said Christina. "And these must be our clothes for the trip." Her expression changed as she held up two plain, scratchy, cotton dresses and two pairs of chocolate-brown work trousers with white shirts.

"Great, real stylish," Christina groaned and carried the larger dress to Mimi. She tried to imagine Mimi in a bland, cotton dress, much different from the trendy clothes and sparkly glasses she usually wore. Christina wondered if Mimi was cut out for life on the open range.

Mimi winked at her granddaughter. "This will be a new look for us," she said. "Isn't 'retro' the new fashion trend these days?"

Grant skipped back to the car to help Papa unload their supplies for the wagon. Papa pulled out blankets, a shovel, a barrel for water, a chest of extra clothes and shoes, and some pots, pans, and plates.

"Where's the TV?" said Grant.

Papa peered at Grant from beneath the brim of his jet-black cowboy hat.

"There's no electricity on the trail, Grant," he explained. "How would you watch TV?"

"I know, Papa," Grant said, smiling mischievously. "I was just joking. That's why I brought my video games with me."

"Video games, huh?" said a gruff voice from behind Grant. Grant slowly turned to see a tall, burly man with tanned, leather skin and a long, curly, gray beard. Grant's eyes grew wide. He looks like someone from a movie, he thought.

"This is supposed to be an authentic trail ride," the man said. "Video games, computers, cell phones, none of that's allowed!" The man looked very annoyed and Grant was about to apologize when another man came walking up.